A Billy Buckhorn Supernatural Adventure

SUPRANORMAL

by Gary Robinson

7th Generation
Summertown, Tennessee

7th Generation, an imprint of
Book Publishing Company
PO Box 99, Summertown, TN 38483
888-260-8458
bookpubco.com
nativevoicesbooks.com

ISBN: 978-1-93905-312-1
20 19 18 17 16 15   1 2 3 4 5 6 7 8 9
Library of Congress Cataloging-in-Publication Data

Robinson, Gary, 1950-
Supranormal : a Billy Buckhorn supernatural adventure / Gary Robinson.
pages cm. -- (Billy Buckhorn supernatural adventures ; 3)
ISBN 978-1-939053-12-1 (pbk.) -- ISBN 978-1-939053-97-8 (e-book)
1. Cherokee Indians--Oklahoma--Fiction. [1. Cherokee Indians--Fiction. 2. Indians of North America--Oklahoma--Fiction. 3. Supernatural--Fiction. 4. Animals, Mythical--Fiction.] I. Title.
PZ7.R56577Su 2015
[Fic]--dc23
2015007692

Book Publishing Company is a member of Green Press Initiative. We chose to print this title on paper with 100% postconsumer recycled content, processed without chlorine, which saved the following natural resources:
• 18 trees
• 563 pounds of solid waste
• 8,414 gallons of water
• 1,551 pounds of greenhouse gases
• 8 million BTU of energy

For more information on Green Press Initiative, visitgreenpressinitiative.org. Environmental impact estimates were made using the Environmental Defense Fund Paper Calculator. For more information visit papercalculator.org.

CONTENTS

THE CONTINUING ADVENTURES OF BILLY BUCKHORN

Billy Buckhorn's exciting story begins in *Abnormal*, when Billy's supernatural abilities become enhanced and he uncovers a frightening secret about an evil teacher's past. After *Paranormal*, the suspension mounts further, as Billy is faced with even greater challenges in *Supranormal*, during which he confronts the dark force that has spread across the Cherokee Nation. Watch for additional volumes in the Billy Buckhorn Supernatural Adventures series, coming soon!

ACKNOWLEDGMENTS

I wish to acknowledge the teachers I've had over the years. Some have been in classrooms. Others were authors of books I read. But many have been people I've met, worked with, or learned from out in the real world. They shared both practical and spiritual knowledge from one human being to another. A few, through their dysfunctional or negative behavior, taught me what not to do and how not to be. No names will be mentioned here.

—*Gary Robinson*

NOTE TO READERS

O-si-yo (hello). You will notice a couple of places in this story where tobacco is used for ceremonial purposes. The use of tobacco in ceremony is an ancient tradition among many tribes. This has nothing to do with the cigarette industry that manufactures addictive, cancer-causing tobacco products. Ceremonial tobacco is used sparingly and is untreated. It is free of chemicals. Used properly, it can be a medium of healing and prayer.

Also, as I noted in *Abnormal* and *Paranormal,* this third book of the Billy Buckhorn series is a work of fiction. However, the story has moved away from the boundaries of Cherokee culture and traditions to a wider scope. In this book, earlier cultures known collectively as the Mound Builders take center stage as the Billy Buckhorn saga continues. Many of today's woodland tribes are descended from these earlier cultures. I hope you enjoy the ride. *Wa-do* (thank you).

—*Gary Robinson*

supranormal: *rising above normal experiences; something that is greater than expected.*

CHAPTER 1
What Next?

A wicked wind whistled through the bare branches above Billy Buckhorn's head. The weather had turned cold in the weeks since Thanksgiving Day. But this was normal for the Cherokee Nation. What wasn't normal was the series of events that had taken place during the past few months. It had definitely been the strangest year of Billy's young life.

On Labor Day, he had been struck by lightning while fishing. Then he began seeing odd visions in his mind. These visions helped the Cherokee teen solve a strange and dangerous mystery. The ghost of Raven Stalker, an evil medicine man who took the form of an oversized raven, had been preying on young victims in the area. Creepy stuff.

Then, on Thanksgiving, Billy and his best friend Chigger discovered an unknown cave. Their exploration of that mysterious place disturbed a colony of bats. In a frenzy of flying fangs and talons, the bats battered Billy as they escaped from the cave. Suffering from dozens of cuts, Billy fell thirty feet and passed out.

Next, as if that wasn't enough, Billy died on the hospital operating table and lived to tell about it. While he was dead, his grandmother Awinita, who had died many years before, visited him. She gave him a choice of staying with her in spirit or going back to continue living on earth. Although there had been something appealing about being "over there," he chose to return to his life here.

On top of all that, the Horned Serpent known as the Uktena, once imprisoned in the bat cave, was now roaming the countryside. This ancient beast was once thought to be just an old Native American myth. The legend of its existence had begun over a thousand years ago. That's when the early Indians known as Mound Builders had first seen the creature.

People who'd seen the serpent said it had antlers like a deer with a diamond in its forehead and a purple crystal at the end of its tail. It was dangerous to both man and animal. If you looked into its eyes, it could hypnotize and even paralyze you.

Some Cherokees said that no one had seen the beast for centuries. Others, including a few medicine people, claimed to have seen it within their lifetimes.

So what could possibly happen next?

That thought flooded Billy's mind as he drove to the Indian hospital. He was on his way to visit Chigger, who was recovering from his own very weird experience. Who could've known that the dark-purple crystal the Cherokee teen had taken from the cave would put him under a spell? That spell had turned Chigger into an angry, ranting maniac. He had held on to the crystal as though it was his own precious possession. But it didn't belong to him, and it wasn't really Chigger doing those things. Someone or something was controlling his mind.

For the time being, the dark crystal was safely hidden away, as were the diamond staff and falcon-feather cape that had once belonged to the now-deceased Falcon Priest. The priest had used the crystal to tame the evil serpent and then he imprisoned the beast in the cave. Billy's grandfather was keeping the dark gem hidden away at his house. The nearby university's archaeologist, Dr. Stevens, had locked the staff and cape in an underground vault. And they would stay hidden away until the right time came, when everything could be arranged and the master plan could be hatched.

Billy stepped into Chigger's hospital room just as a nurse was leaving. Chigger's mother, Molly Muskrat, sat in a chair next to the bed watching her son. Chigger was sitting up in bed, eating pudding from a cup. He was having trouble holding the spoon and the cup because both his hands were bandaged. A third gauze bandage was wrapped around the boy's head. He looked like a scary character from an old horror movie.

"Don't you think it's a little late for Halloween?" Billy said. Chigger and his mother turned to see who had come into the room. "You look like you're dressed up as The Mummy," he added.

"Billy!" Chigger exclaimed. "I wondered when you were going to find time to visit your oldest best friend." He put the spoon and cup down on the tray.

"We're so glad you came," Mrs. Muskrat said, standing up. "Your mother said you might be stopping by today."

Billy's mother was a nurse at the same hospital.

Standing near the bed, Billy reached out and pulled his friend close. They hugged.

"This is awkward," Chigger said jokingly when Billy held his friend for what seemed like a long time. "You're going to make Sara jealous."

That made Billy let go.

"I'm breaking up with her," Billy said seriously. "Right after I leave here."

"What? Are you kidding me?" Chigger asked. To Chigger, this was good news, although he'd never say that to Billy.

"I'm serious," Billy replied. "You know how I hate outside attention or publicity."

"Yeah, I know it all too well," Chigger said. "You've never taken me up on my offer to be your agent and get you on a reality TV show. But what does that have to do with Sara?"

"Well, she's become a social-media freak," Billy said. "She's built an online fan club of friends who follow her because she's the girlfriend of the famous Lightning Boy."

"How'd you find this out?" Chigger asked. "You don't have a Facebook page."

"My mother does," Billy said. "She's online all the time. She told me about it."

Chigger had always known that Billy's mom was on his side. Go, Mrs. Buckhorn!

"That's too bad," Chigger said, acting all sad. "You need to be with someone who appreciates you for you, not your special abilities."

"Yeah, well, don't lay it on too thick, Chigger," Billy said. "I know you never liked her."

"Whatever," Chigger replied.

"So tell me what happened with the dark crystal," Billy said. His tone was serious again.

"Grandpa Wesley and I are trying to understand how it works. You're a firsthand witness to its power."

"I'm afraid I can't help you," Chigger replied. "My mind's a blank. The last thing I remember is coming to your house for a visit. You were recovering from your fall at the cave and dying on the operating table. In fact, you were all bandaged up, looking like this." He gestured to his own hands and head.

"That's too bad. I was hoping for some clues."

Then something clicked in Chigger's mind.

"Now that I think of it, I do remember having a sort of weird dream," Chigger said. "It seemed to go on and on forever."

"What was it?" Billy sat on the edge of the bed.

"I was moving through water, just gliding along," Chigger said. "I looked down at my body, and it looked like I was a big snake. I mean really big. Then I saw my reflection in the water. And I had antlers. Like deer antlers."

"You saw the beast!" Billy said excitedly. "You were under its spell."

"If you say so."

"Anything else?" Billy asked.

"It felt like I was searching for something," Chigger answered. "Something very important that had been stolen from me. Whatever it was, it belonged to me."

"The diamond from the Falcon Priest's staff."

"The what on the who?" Chigger said.

"The brilliant gemstone that used to be fixed to the Horned Serpent's forehead."

Billy saw the very puzzled look on Chigger's face.

"A lot has happened since you and I came out of that cave, Chigger. A lot."

Billy quickly gave him a rundown of the events: The trip back to the cave with the experts. The withered grass and bushes along the trail at the Spiral Mounds site. The curious hole in the side of one of the mounds. The discovery of the Falcon Priest's cape and staff.

"Get well soon," Billy said when he'd finished his story. "I want you with us when we return to the cave to recapture the serpent.

Maybe we can use the bond you had with the beast to help us draw him back."

Chigger eagerly agreed to help out however he could. Just before Billy left, Chigger wished him good luck with Sara.

Now it was time for Billy to face his girlfriend, or rather, his soon-to-be former girlfriend. They had only been seeing each other since right after he'd saved Sara from the claws of Raven Stalker, the evil medicine man Billy had confronted in September. Billy had never had a girlfriend before that. But he soon learned that girlfriends expect things—things like time and attention and promises. Billy realized he wasn't ready for any of it.

"Billy!" Sara yelled when she saw him across the high school parking lot. He'd timed his arrival at the school so he'd be waiting for her when school was out. Billy hadn't been in class much lately. His mother had complained about it, but there were too many things to do. Too many people to see. Too many preparations for events to come. There would be plenty of time for school later.

Sara ran to the truck and climbed in the passenger door. She leaned over, expecting a kiss. But Billy had other plans. He took a deep breath.

"Sara, I'm breaking up with you," he blurted out.

Sara responded with stunned silence. That was rare for this girl. Billy continued.

"I saw your Facebook page and read all the comments you posted," he said sternly. "Over and over, you brag like you're the girlfriend of a big-shot celebrity. You use me to get friends and boost your popularity. It makes me feel like a circus freak. I want out!"

Anger filled her eyes. Panic ran through her veins. How dare he ruin her climbing social status! How could he be so selfish to not think of her needs! Then she realized what she was thinking. She listened to what she was saying in her mind. And she thought of what she'd been doing.

"Billy Buckhorn, you're the most incredible human being I know," she said. Tears began to form in her eyes.

"Sara, don't—"

"Shut up and listen," she demanded. "I will never be half the person you are. All I have are my little shares, likes, and selfies to give to the world. That's all."

"No, don't say that," Billy responded. "I know you've got— "

"Stop interrupting!"

Billy fell silent. Sara recomposed herself.

"I want to be somebody some day," she continued. "This is the only way I know how."

"You saw that thing, that creature, in the plant nursery," Billy reminded her. "You saw how it shifted and changed from a man into an evil bird thing. It was about to suck the very life out of you."

"I know," she admitted. "I try to forget it, but I can't erase those images from my mind."

"That sort of thing seems to be a permanent part of my life now," Billy said. "There's no turning back for me. I've been called into action, and I'm going to answer that call. I'm obviously not going to lead a normal life."

Sara looked into Billy's eyes. For the first time she really saw the depth there. It was the same depth Billy's father had seen before. Now she understood. She finally got what Billy was all about.

"Friends?" she asked putting out her hand. "I mean real friends, not the Facebook kind."

"Friends," Billy responded, shaking on it. Before letting go, he lifted her hand and kissed it. "Thanks for understanding," he said.

Sara raised her index finger to her lips and kissed it. Then she placed that finger in the middle of the spiderlike scar on the side of Billy's neck, just like she'd done when she had thanked him for saving her life.

Smiling and holding back tears, the girl opened the truck door and climbed out. She waved to Billy and turned away. Then, as her ex-boyfriend drove away, her tears flowed freely. The bottom fell out of her heart, and she knew there would never be another boy in her life like Billy Buckhorn.

CHAPTER 2
A Pile of Bones

Saturday was Grandpa Wesley's busiest day as a Cherokee medicine man. His doctoring skills were known far and wide. Even though Native medicine men weren't part of the medical establishment, their people called them doctors. Using methods long kept secret, they would prepare, or "doctor," herbs to help heal their patients.

On Saturdays, people began lining up early in hopes of seeing Wesley. He didn't make appointments. As with most Native medicine people, it was first come, first served.

Billy knew the time was fast approaching when he'd be taking over his grandfather's practice. But he still had a lot to learn about Cherokee medicines, songs, and healing techniques. Saturdays were when he went to help the elder out and get more lessons in the process.

As Billy pulled up in front of Wesley's white frame house, he noticed that the line of waiting patients seemed to be longer than usual. A few of the patients spotted Billy and moved toward him as he got out of the truck.

He could see the need in their eyes. This used to scare him a little when he came to help his grandfather. Wesley always took care of that need. Then Billy became famous for his psychic abilities, saving a busload of children, and stopping a child predator. People started turning more of that need toward him. Many would reach out just to touch him as he passed, like he was a saint or a miracle worker to them. That really shook him up.

But Wesley had reminded Billy of how healing works. It was a person's own faith that did much of the work. Their own inner belief opened the channels. The healing was already there and available. But faith often allowed a person to receive it.

So this morning, Billy allowed the waiting people to touch him. He smiled as he passed, speaking softly to them. "*Osiyo. To-hit-su?*" he said in Cherokee, words his grandfather had taught him. "Hello. How are you?" he followed up in English. "*Osda sunalei. To-hi-du,*" he said to someone else. "Good morning. May you have peace of mind, body, and spirit."

"Words of kindness," Wesley said to Billy as the boy stepped up on the porch. "That's what this world needs." The elder welcomed his grandson into the house. "We'll begin in just a few minutes," Wesley announced to everyone in Cherokee. "Please be patient."

The elder and his grandson stepped inside the house. Wesley knew that Billy had just come from Chigger's hospital room.

"Well, what did he have to say?" Wesley asked as he poured them both a cup of coffee from a dented old pot. "Could Chigger tell you any more about it?"

Billy repeated his friend's sudden memory of seeing things through the serpent's eyes. Wesley agreed that this could help them with their plans to recapture the beast.

"I've never seen anything like what's happening in the Nation now," Wesley said, looking out the kitchen window. "A dark force has spread across the land like a heavy blanket.

I can see it in people's eyes. They're scared and confused."

He turned to Billy. "Can you help me out today?" he asked.

"Of course, Grandpa," Billy answered. "What do you need me to do?"

"It won't be pleasant," Wesley warned.

"I can handle it," Billy said, taking a gulp of coffee.

"Okay. I want you to go with Mr. and Mrs. Kingfisher back to their place. They live near Caney Creek on the other side of the lake. Their small dog was attacked by some unknown creature. All that's left of their pet is a pile of bones."

"It was probably just a mountain lion or large wolf that came down from the hills," Billy said. That happened sometimes in the rural areas of eastern Oklahoma.

"There was no blood," Wesley said. "There were no body parts either. Just a pile of bones picked clean."

"How's that possible?" Billy asked. "That's *not* possible."

"That's why I want you to go check it out," Wesley said. "Look around and tell me what you see. Put the bones in a bag and bring them to me."

"Yet another mystery," Billy said as he stood to leave.

"Before you go, I want to show you one more thing," Wesley said. "Follow me out to the woods behind the house."

Stepping out the back door, Wesley headed through his backyard herb garden. Billy followed. Seeing the garden reminded him of someone.

"Where's Little Wolf been lately?" Billy asked. "I haven't seen him around."

Little Wolf was one of the Little People, the small helper spirits who lived in the woods.

"I sent him on a special long-distance mission," Wesley said. "He probably won't be back for a couple more weeks."

Opening the back gate, Wesley continued across the field behind his house. That's when Billy realized that his grandfather wasn't using his cane. And he was moving faster than he'd ever seen him move.

"What happened to your cane?" Billy asked. "And your hurt leg?"

Wesley stopped in his tracks and turned to his grandson.

"You don't know about Wilma, do you?" he said with a smile.

"Who's Wilma?"

"She's one of the medicine people who helped me get the crystal from Chigger," Wesley replied. "She asked me over for dinner the other day. Let's keep moving."

The elder began walking again.

"She's quite an amazing woman," Wesley said.

Billy heard a hint of something in the old man's voice that he hadn't heard before. He almost sounded like a teenager. Billy's grandpa had a crush! How interesting.

"Turns out she's not only a medicine healer, but also a gifted physical therapist," Wesley continued. "She located a place on my spine that was twisted. It was pinching the nerve to my leg. She untwisted it, and now I feel like my old self."

They arrived at their destination, a shed that stood at the edge of the woods. Billy had a strange look on his face.

"What?" Wesley asked. "Did I say something funny?"

Billy merely shook his head and smiled.

"You mean now you feel like your *young* self, don't you?" Billy said with a raised eyebrow.

"Whatever," Grandpa replied, turning his attention to the shed. A large padlock hung from a latch that secured the door. Taking a key from his pocket, Wesley opened the lock. He pulled the shed door open to reveal an old bank safe inside. Script letters spelling "Rockwell Bank" had been painted on its side long ago.

"What's this?" Billy said. "Where'd you get it?"

"From an auction in town," Wesley said as he turned the dial on the front of the safe. "It's where I keep important stuff."

"Like what?" Billy asked as Wesley opened the door wide.

"Like the dark crystal we took from Chigger. And the old *Cherokee Medicine Book.*"

Grandpa removed a leather bag from a shelf in the safe. He set the bag down on the ground and opened the bag's flap.

"Look, but don't touch," Wesley instructed.

Billy peered into the bag and saw the glowing purple crystal resting at the bottom.

"Is it my imagination, or is that thing brighter than it used to be?" Billy said.

"It's not your imagination," Wesley replied. "It's been growing brighter every day."

He folded the flap closed and put the bag back in the safe.

"What does it mean?" Billy asked.

"I think it means the Horned Serpent is getting closer," Wesley said. "I think it means we have to act soon, before it finds this."

Wesley closed and locked the safe, then he closed and locked the shed door.

"That's why I want you to go out to the Kingfishers' place," Wesley said as he and Billy headed back to the house. "I'm afraid the Uktena got their dog. And that would mean that he is getting close."

CHAPTER 3
Judge Not

Billy followed Mr. and Mrs. Kingfisher to their home to see the pile of bones. They lived near a creek that emptied into Lake Tenkiller. Billy knew this lake was connected to the Illinois River and then to the Arkansas River. That river had taken Chigger and him to the cave where the Horned Serpent had been trapped.

Mr. Kingfisher led Billy around to the back of the house. There, in a far corner of the yard, lay the pile of small bones that had once been their little dog. Billy knew at once that the dog had become a meal for the beast. There were telltale signs, including a trail of withered grass and bushes that led from the creek to the yard. It was the same kind of withered trail they had found at Spiral Mounds, the ancient Native burial site near the cave where the serpent had been imprisoned.

Billy asked the elderly Mr. and Mrs. Kingfisher to come stand with him. Together they formed a little circle around the bones. He said a Cherokee prayer for their dog, which they had named Warrior. Warrior had been their guard for many years, even though he wasn't much larger than a fat house cat. Billy said the prayer to help the elderly couple mourn their longtime protector. He didn't say anything about the beast that had surely eaten their little friend.

Next, he gathered up the bones and put them in a bag to take back to his grandfather. He sprinkled tobacco around the area where the bones had been. Then he gave the Kingfishers a packet of tobacco that Wesley had doctored.

"If you hear anything suspicious back here, offer this tobacco to the four directions and say a prayer for protection," Billy told them. The old couple thanked him for his services, and Mrs. Kingfisher sent him off with a plate of homemade cookies.

In a short while he was back at Wesley's to report what he'd seen.

"There's no doubt he's headed this way," Wesley said. "He's coming for the dark crystal. We'd better get together with your father and

Dr. Stevens soon. We have to set our plan in motion before it's too late."

Billy agreed to talk to his dad about setting things up when he got home that night. The boy spent the rest of the day helping Wesley look after the physical and emotional needs of his patients. Almost everyone had some strange story to tell—unusual happenings, missing animals, ghost sightings, withered plants, depressed feelings. The list went on and on.

Drained by the day's activities, Billy arrived home in time to have dinner with his mom and dad.

"Your uncle John wants to come by this evening to see you," Mrs. Buckhorn said at the dinner table.

"Oh no, not him," Billy complained. "I don't think I can handle any preaching tonight from your brother the reverend."

"He promised not to preach this time," she replied.

"That's what he said last time," Billy said.

"He knows it will be the last time he sees any of us if he breaks his promise," his mom said. "I think he was really shaken up the last time he was here. Now he wants to apologize."

"That man isn't capable of making an apology," Billy's dad said. "He's too self-righteous to ever do that."

"He's my brother, and I think we should at least give him a chance," Mrs. Buckhorn said. "I promise to kick him out if he even so much as hints at preaching."

Billy just looked at her and sighed.

"I promise," she said again.

"Okay," Billy said as he finished his last bite of food. "What time is he coming?"

Before his mother could answer, there came a loud knock at the front door.

"I guess right about now," she said, getting up from the table.

They all moved to the living room as Billy's uncle, John Ross, stepped inside behind Billy's mother.

"I've come to ask for your help, Billy," the preacher said. "But first I have something to tell you."

Billy stood across the room as far away from the man as possible. There was just no telling what he might say or do.

"Jesus said judge not, lest ye be judged," the preacher said.

"You said no preaching," Billy's mother complained.

"I'm not preaching," John replied, looking at his sister. "I'm confessing. Just give me a minute."

He turned back to Billy.

"Jesus told us not to judge other people so we wouldn't be judged harshly by God," the preacher said. "But all I've done is judge. You, your father, and your grandfather. I pointed a finger at what I thought was wrong with all of you. I see now that I should've been trying to fix myself."

"Okay," Billy said, not sure where this was going.

"You shined a light on the lie I'd been living with all my life," John admitted. "You revealed the truth about my responsibility for the death of my brother, Luther. I am ashamed, and I ask for your forgiveness. The forgiveness of all of you in this household."

"We can neither condemn you nor forgive you," Billy's dad said. "But we can accept your apology. Right, Billy?"

"Yeah, sure," Billy replied. "Is that all you wanted?"

"No, I want to ask you for a favor," John said. "Even though I'd understand if you didn't want to do it."

"Grandpa Wesley taught me to always help another Cherokee whenever asked," Billy said. "Now you've asked, so I will help you if I can."

"Thank you," John said. He moved further into the living room. Billy moved a little closer to his uncle, as well.

"Can you give my brother, Luther, a message for me?" John asked in a quiet tone. "I'm not sure how your communication with the spirits of the dead works."

"I'm still trying to figure that out myself," Billy replied honestly. "But I will if I can. What would you like me to tell him?"

"Just that I'm sorry," the preacher said. "Sorry that he suffered because of my carelessness. Sorry that I never took responsibility for my actions. Sorry that he never got to live his full life. That's all."

"All right, Uncle, I'll pass along the message the next chance I get," Billy offered. "I don't know when that'll be, but I'll get it done."

"Thank you," John replied, rushing to shake Billy's hand. "I'd be forever grateful."

After pumping his nephew's hand a few times and saying his good-byes to everyone, Billy's uncle left.

"That wasn't so bad, now was it?" Billy's mother commented. "I think he's a changed man."

"Yeah, but how long will the change last?" Billy's father said. "I'll wait to see how he acts at the next family dinner before letting my guard down."

"I think he's sincere," Billy said. "When I shook his hand, I didn't sense any false feelings or see any bad images."

"I thought your ability to see what was going on inside people had faded," his mother said.

"It comes and goes," Billy replied as he headed back to the kitchen in search of dessert.

What Billy didn't realize is that the message had already been passed to Luther. Billy was an active channel to the spirit world without even knowing it. Ever since his near-death experience, the souls of the departed lingered nearby. Many hoped to send messages to their loved ones on earth.

A couple of hours after he went to bed, Billy woke up to find his grandmother Awinita standing near the foot of his bed. She was in her glowing spirit form, as usual. But she wasn't alone. Standing beside her was the spirit of Billy's great-grandfather, Bullseye Buckhorn. He'd been given that name a hundred years ago, when he was a young man, because he was the best with a blowgun in the Cherokee Nation.

"You can tell your uncle John that Luther got the message," Awinita said, though she didn't actually speak. Her words were transferred from her mind to Billy's.

"Luther thinks it certainly took his stubborn brother a long time to admit the truth," Bullseye added. “But he was glad John finally did. How are you doing, Billy?”

“Fine, Great-grandpa,” Billy said. “I didn’t expect to see you.”

“I’ve been hanging out more with Awinita lately,” he replied.

“What’s going on, Grandma?” Billy asked. “I know you two didn’t show up just to tell me what Uncle Luther had to say.”

“I sent your great-grandfather on a scouting trip, and he’s here to tell you what he found,” Awinita replied.

“I’ve been to hell and back,” Bullseye said with a smile and a twinkle in his eye.

“What?” Billy said and blinked, not understanding what his great-grandfather meant.

“Well, hell isn’t really what humans think it is,” he said. “Or where they think it is. You see—”

“No time for that now,” Billy’s grandmother said, interrupting him. “Get on with it.”

“Oh, well, maybe another time, young man,” Bullseye said. “Like your grandma said, she sent me to the lower realms of the spirit world. There was a disturbance coming from there that we in the higher realms could feel."

"You can do that?" Billy asked. "Move from area to area?"

"Oh yes," Bullseye said. "Residents of the higher regions can visit the lower layers, not that you'd really want to. But it doesn't work the other way around. It's a matter of energy vibrations, like tuning in a radio station."

That went over Billy's head. He was still getting used to the whole talking-to-dead-people thing. And he still didn't really understand much of it.

"Are you going to get to the point or am I going to have to get there for you?" Awinita insisted.

"I'll make a long story short," Bullseye said. "It's a frenzy of dark energy down there. And the reason is this. When the Horned Serpent awoke, his revived energy was noticed. Ancient minions had been assigned to watch over the beast so they could report any signs of his awakening."

"Minions? What are minions?" Billy asked.

"They're followers," Awinita answered. "They do the bidding of someone of great power. In the Underworld, they're like small, dark ghost creatures."

"Okay. Who do these minions answer to?" Billy asked.

"In this case, the Dark Priest," Bullseye said.

"I've never heard of the Dark Priest," Billy said. "But he doesn't sound good."

"He isn't!" Bullseye said. "The Dark Priest led a cult of Horned Serpent worshippers during the Mound Builder period. The Falcon Priest threw them out of their villages. He wouldn't allow their evil intentions to take hold of his followers."

"Why did anyone follow the Dark Priest if he was so bad?" Billy asked.

"The same reason anyone gets involved with the dark side," Awinita answered. "Power. Power over people. Power to make things happen the way you want them to happen."

"Anyway, the Dark Priest has reconnected with the Horned Serpent, and it's bad news," Bullseye said. "He is able to guide the beast from the other side. Help him along his quest to regain the diamond and the purple crystal."

"If his power is anything like what I saw with Benjamin Blacksnake, then it is bad news," Billy said. "It's nothing but death and destruction."

"You are so very lucky, young man, that Blacksnake—the most evil medicine man who ever lived—didn't have a chance to suck the very life out of you," Bullseye said. "Why he could've—"

"So you know what's at stake here," Billy's grandmother interrupted. "If the Dark Priest is controlling the Horned Serpent—"

"And if the serpent's powers are restored through the two gems—" Bullseye continued.

"Then the Uktena will become unstoppable!" Billy concluded.

CHAPTER 4
Slithering Forth

The Great Snake had grown weary from his travels. It was both exciting and tiring to be out in the world again, free from that liquid prison at the bottom of the cave. Free to roam the land and take what he needed, whenever he needed it. It had been so long since he had that kind of freedom.

After first leaving the cave, the beast had floated down the Arkansas River. The river current had gently carried him along. Little effort was required, and it was familiar territory. He had roamed this region freely. Long ago, he could drift downstream until the Arkansas River met the Mississippi River, which, of course, flowed directly to the ocean.

When he had left the cave, he immediately felt a strong pull in two opposite directions. The strongest pull had been from the south, so that's where the creature had gone first. The beast was sure that's where the diamond could be found.

The serpent's attraction to the diamond was a longing for his past glory. That gem had once lived in his forehead, and the clear stone was indeed a living thing. It throbbed with a life force. And it had shone brightly when it was in its place. It gave him incredible power over all living things.

In those days, the beast's only friend was a leader of the two-legged ones. He was known as the Dark Priest. His powers came from the Underworld, the same place that the Uktena had come from. The Dark Priest had power over other humans. He formed the Serpent Cult, and they all worshipped the beast.

But the one called the Falcon Priest had defeated the Dark Priest. It had been a bloody battle that the humans remembered for a long time. The Falcon Priest had powers of his own. He used those powers to defeat his enemy and to learn the dark secret: the secret of subduing the serpent by hypnotizing it. The Dark Priest revealed this secret just before he was executed.

And the Falcon Priest used this secret to conquer the serpent. That's when the beast was imprisoned in the cave.

But, like all humans, the Falcon Priest also died. That was so long ago. The beast had no real way of measuring time. And the diamond had been buried with that human in those mounds. That's what had attracted the beast to that place.

The serpent arrived at the Spiral Mounds in the dark of night. But his eyes were used to the dark. And he knew he had come to the right place. He felt the diamond. It throbbed from underground. Like a lighthouse, the diamond sent out its invisible beacon into the night.

The beast began happily digging up that gem. But he had to stop when a two-legged one showed up. In the old days, when the diamond lived in his forehead, its light would have blinded the man. Paralyzed him. But this man carried his own light. When the light from his hand shined on the serpent's scales, it bounced back. Its reflection blinded the man because the beast's scales contained a little of the diamond's power. But the blinding would only be temporary.

Then a loud noise had burst forth from all around the mound area. Wailing screeched across the darkness and a barrage of lights lit up the night. The beast was not familiar with modern-day sirens and emergency lights.

Startled by the sound and the brightness, the beast was forced to flee the mounds without his prize. He headed quickly back to the safety of the river. Underwater was where he actually belonged, where his ancestors had come from. So that's where he hid until he felt safe again.

That's when the ghost of the Dark Priest again made contact with the serpent after all that lost time. The beast had been in a deep sleep, unable to see, hear, or feel anything or anyone. So the Dark Priest had not been able to speak to him.

But now the Dark One had finally found a way to contact the physical world. From his mind to the beast's mind, the priest spoke the ancient words. But he could only do so from mind to mind. The Dark Priest was unable to speak the words aloud.

The mental words had only a small effect. He could not fully reunite with the Uktena. So the ghost had to be content with guiding the snake in his search for the diamond and the purple gem. He was able to help the snake be more sensitive to the signals coming from these stones. He could also watch and wait. Maybe, when the beast found the stones, the Dark Priest's powers would also be strengthened.

A few days later, the serpent returned to the mound. But the diamond was gone. It had been taken. Again it had been snatched from him by two-leggeds. The beast had felt it move away from that place. Northward.

The whole time the beast was in the south searching for the diamond, the dark crystal also called to him. It was already in the north. The young two-legged one took it from the cave. The beast knew it was a young one who had the stone because the Dark Priest had used his supernatural force to create a visible connection between it and the beast. The serpent could see through the eyes of anyone who held his precious crystal. And the beast could see who held it as well. It was definitely a young two-legged one. And he saw other older two-legged ones who came. They had come to take that crystal from him.

The young one would not give up the stone without a fight. But finally the boy had been surrounded by four of the two-leggeds with their own weak powers. The four of them together were powerful enough to steal it away.

The number four. It was indeed a sad day all those centuries ago when the two-legged ones learned the power of four. The number four stood for the Four Great Forces that flowed through the physical world. It had been hidden from the weak humans in the early days. But as the knowledge of the two-leggeds had increased, so had their ability to trap the beast.

But at last the time had come. Now both the diamond and the dark crystal were near each other. Closer to each other than they'd been in ages. So the serpent had begun his northward journey, swimming upstream, fighting the river current to attain his goal. Soon he would rejoin the diamond to his forehead and reattach the purple stone to his tail. Then he would be complete again. Whole.

Of course, he had to keep up his strength during the journey. That's why he would leave the safety of the river from time to time, slithering across the land. A small creature now and then would become a meal. But only the flesh and muscles and tissues. Never the bones. His system couldn't digest the bones so those were left behind.

And then it was time to move on. Ever onward toward the goal, toward the final reunion with his precious possessions and his power.

And the unseen ghost of the Dark Priest was there every moment of the journey.

CHAPTER 5
The Missing Piece

The following day Billy drove to Chigger's mobile home to pick him up. The bandages on Chigger's hands were smaller now and the bandage on his head was gone. All in all, Chigger looked pretty good.

They then drove to the campus of the nearby college, where Billy's dad, professor James Buckhorn, taught courses in Cherokee history and culture. When they arrived at the professor's office, Billy's father and grandfather were waiting for them.

Spread on the professor's desk were photos and notes. These had been taken several weeks earlier when Billy, his dad, his grandfather, and Dr. Stevens had explored the cave.

"The pieces of the cave puzzle seem to be coming together," Billy's dad said as Chigger and Billy sat down. "Grandpa told me about the pile of bones you found."

"Now we need to review what the Falcon Priest said about recapturing the beast," Grandpa added. "That way all of us will know what to expect when we try to trap the beast back in the cave."

"Where's Dr. Stevens?" Billy asked. "I thought he was supposed to be here."

"Is he the digger you told me about?" Chigger asked. He hadn't met the archaeologist who had gone with the team to explore the cave and Spiral Mounds.

"He doesn't like being called a digger," Billy's dad told Chigger. "It's not a dignified name."

"In case you hadn't noticed, I ain't so dignified myself," Chigger replied. "But okay."

"Anyway, he's probably just running late," the professor said. "I think we can start without him."

"I really don't know what I can do to help," Chigger said. "Each of you has a part to play."

"And you do, too," Billy replied. "You have a connection to the Horned Serpent that no one else does. You've seen him from the inside out."

"I hadn't thought of it that way," Chigger said. "Glad to be of service."

Professor Buckhorn shuffled through the photos on his desk. Finally he found the one he was looking for. It was a shot of the stone door that had sealed the serpent in the lake. On its surface were the markings Billy and Chigger had first seen on the day that Billy died.

"Tell us again what the spirit of the Falcon Priest told you about these markings," the professor said to his son. "When we were at Spiral Mounds."

"He said the symbols were the letters of a special language used by their holy people," Billy explained. "And what was written there were the words that must be spoken to capture the serpent and hold him in that cave."

"How are you supposed to say those words?" Chigger asked. "You don't speak their language."

"The Falcon Priest said he would speak those words through me at the right moment," Billy replied. "He said he would take over my mind and body with my grandmother Awinita's help."

"You're kidding me, right?" Chigger said in disbelief. "Some dude who died a thousand years ago is gonna show up at just the right time. And then he's gonna use your vocal chords to say some magic words?"

"You're questioning me about what happened at Spiral Mounds?" Billy said with a note of sarcasm. "Oh, that's right. You weren't with us. At that time you were possessed by the power of an evil snake that made you go crazy. And it took four people to get the dark crystal out of your hands."

"When you put it that way," Chigger admitted, "what you said is totally believable."

"But before those words can be spoken, we have many things to do to get ready," Billy continued. "First we have to return the purple gem to its place near the stone door. And this is where you come in, Chigger."

Chigger sat up straight in his chair, glad to be an important part of the team.

"The person who removed the gem must be the one who replaces it," Billy said.

Chigger slumped back down in his chair, realizing that he was the one who caused this whole mess to begin with. If he hadn't left the cave with that stone, they might not be facing all this trouble.

"Then we wait and watch," Billy's dad said. "The serpent will get a mental signal telling him the stone is back in its place. And he'll probably feel the presence of the diamond in the same area. He'll head back for the cave."

"Once the beast is inside the cave, Billy will enter," Wesley said. "He'll be wearing the Falcon Priest's cape and holding the diamond staff."

"The Horned Serpent should be focused on finding the dark crystal so he can reattach it to his tail," Billy said. "So I'll follow him down the path toward the lake at the bottom of the cave."

"When he sees the diamond that Billy will be carrying, the beast will become hypnotized," the professor said. "Billy can lead him beyond the stone door and back into the lake."

"That's when the sacred words must be spoken," Wesley said. "The stone door will close and reseal itself. The beast will be a prisoner once again."

"It's all pretty simple," Billy said with a smile. "Simple as one, two, three."

"Oh, and there's no way anything can go wrong," Chigger said with his own hint of sarcasm. "You guys are nuts. This'll never work."

"Thanks for your vote of confidence," Billy replied. "Do you—"

Before Billy could complete his sentence, his father's desk phone rang.

"Professor Buckhorn," James said, then listened for a moment.

"Oh my God," he said finally. "We'll be right there."

"That was Dr. Stevens," he said as he slammed down the receiver. "He's been attacked by the serpent, and his artifact collection was destroyed."

Everyone froze in place for a long moment. This took them completely by surprise.

"What are we waiting for?" Chigger said as he jumped up. "We've gotta get a move on."

Everyone rose at once.

"We can all fit in my car," James said. "It's parked just outside."

Silently, they followed the professor out the door.

Dr. Stevens lived east of the college campus in a house that bordered the Illinois River. The river spilled directly into Lake Tenkiller, so the serpent would have easy access to the house from the water.

When the team pulled up in front of the archaeologist's home, there were no signs of an attack. As they approached the front door, a Native woman in a nurse's uniform opened it and greeted them.

"Dr. Stevens asked me to meet you at the door," she said. "He's resting in his bedroom, but it's all right for you to go back and see him."

"Will he be okay?" Billy's dad asked as the team entered the house. "Is he hurt badly?"

"He's mostly dazed and confused," the nurse replied. "I think—"

The nurse was interrupted by a booming voice coming from the back of the house.

"Billy Buckhorn, I owe you a huge apology," Dr. Stevens said as he came toward them. His face was covered with small cuts and scrapes. One eye was bandaged.

"Dr. Stevens, you shouldn't be out of bed," the nurse scolded. "You heard what the doctor said."

"Yeah, yeah, yeah," Stevens replied. "I can rest when I'm dead. I've got a lot to share with these gentlemen."

"Well, don't be too long," she replied as she turned away. "I'll be in the kitchen if you need me."

"You guys have got to see this," Dr. Stevens said with excitement. "Follow me to my office."

He led them to a door at the rear of the house. As he stepped outside, Billy could see the river, along with a trail of dead, withered plants leading from the river to the house.

Stevens started climbing down a set of stairs and the group followed him. They ended up in a basement. It was a total mess. Furniture was overturned and shelving from the walls lay in pieces on the floor. Shattered fragments of pottery, stones, and baskets were scattered all around.

Ignoring the ruins that were once his office, Dr. Stevens first addressed Billy's father.

"We scholars and academics have it all wrong," he said, his eyes wide with astonishment. "These tribal legends aren't just old stories made up by primitive peoples to explain things they didn't understand. Now I know that at least some of these are based on actual truths."

Billy and the others walked carefully through the room. Destroyed Native American artifacts and documents were strewn everywhere.

"What are you talking about?" Billy's father demanded. "Why aren't you concerned about the destruction of your collection?"

"Because *I saw* the Horned Serpent with my own eyes," Dr. Stevens answered. "What before had only been a curious myth came bursting through that door in real life! I was saved from certain death only because of what I was studying at that moment."

He began searching through a pile of rubble at the back of the room.

"I know it's here somewhere," he said as he sorted through a stack of scattered papers. "Ah, here it is."

He withdrew a large color photo from the pile. It was tattered at the edges and covered with dust. He wiped it off and held it up for them all to see.

"It's the eye-in-hand symbol," he said proudly. "This image has been found at many of the Mound Builder sites."

Billy looked at the photo. In the center was the open palm of a man's hand. In the middle of the palm was an eye. The hand was surrounded on all sides by two horned snakes woven together. They'd been tied in knots. It seemed to mean the snakes were under control.

"This eye-in-hand image has also been found in ancient Jewish and Hindu sites in the Middle East and India," Billy's father observed.

"What does it mean?" Chigger asked.

"My research says it's a way to connect to the Upperworld, or what we call heaven," Dr. Stevens said. "It's the eye of God, and it's in our hands. The serpents are the symbol for the Underworld. They're tied up, so they're harmless."

"Okay, so how did this picture save you from the monster thingy?" Chigger said, bringing the group firmly back to the present.

"The beast came crashing through those doors last night," Stevens explained. "It moved quickly through the room, turning over objects and breaking my prized artifacts. But I could tell it was looking for something. It was desperate."

"The diamond staff!" Billy suddenly blurted. "Of course, the serpent knew it was here. Don't tell me he got it!"

"No, thankfully, he didn't," Dr. Stevens said. "At first, I thought you were crazy when you started talking about the Falcon Priest at

Spiral Mounds. You said you got some kind of message from the spirit world about the serpent myth. But I decided to hide the cape and staff in my underground vault just in case you weren't out of your mind."

"But finish the story of what happened when the beast came crashing in here!" Chigger demanded. "I'm dying to find out."

Dr. Stevens took the eye-in-hand photo from Chigger.

"I was examining this very image as the beast was rushing toward me," he said. "I figured I was about to be killed. But silly me, I held this photo up over my head and crouched down on the floor. I guess it was just instinct to hold something up for protection."

He knelt down on the floor to demonstrate what he'd done.

"It was just a piece of paper, right?" Dr. Stevens continued. "It obviously couldn't have stopped the beast from tearing right through it and biting my head off."

Then he stood up.

"But that *did* stop it," he said calmly. "The serpent was repelled by the image. Its eyes grew wide, and it jumped back. It tried moving to one side and coming at me from a different angle. I swung the photo around and held it like a shield."

"Amazing," Billy's dad said.

"Soon the beast realized he couldn't get to me," Dr. Stevens said. "I even felt a little brave and took a few steps toward him. And he turned and slithered away at top speed."

"This is a missing piece of the puzzle," Billy said with confidence. "From now on, each of us needs to have a copy of this symbol. If we're going to confront the serpent, we should have it on us at all times. For protection."

"So you understand why I'm apologizing," Stevens said. "These are no mere myths. These are warnings. People really experienced some of this stuff. That means that at least a few of the tribal legends are true. Maybe things were added as the stories were passed along. But they're rooted in reality. I know that now."

CHAPTER 6
One More Step

Billy was amazed at how both his father and Dr. Stevens had changed their minds about Native legends. These two college big-brains finally came to believe what he and Grandpa had known all along: that many fantastic ancient Native American stories contained truths at their core.

"Why don't we just shoot the thing the next time we see it?" Chigger suggested. "Or stab it or spear it or cut its head off?"

"If it were only that simple," Wesley replied. "Its scales can't be pierced. At least that's what the *Cherokee Medicine Book* says. And so do all the oral stories passed down through the generations."

"It's the perfect monster," Chigger observed. "You can't kill it, and it lives forever. Kind of like Godzilla. Just when you think it's gone for good, boom! It resurrects and attacks."

They all had a good laugh at that one, a much-needed release of some of the tension brewed by the gravity of their situation.

Before leaving Dr. Stevens's home, the group helped him straighten up his office, at least as much as they could. Dr. Stevens said that many priceless artifacts had been destroyed. But he didn't focus on the loss like he would have in the past. Now all he wanted to do was be a part of the crew that resealed the beast in the bottom of the cave.

So that made the team complete. It consisted of Billy, his dad, his grandfather Wesley, Chigger, and Dr. Stevens, who now insisted on being called by his first name, Augustus.

"What a team," Chigger said as they drove back to campus. "We're like supernatural superheroes. We could call ourselves the . . . what's a good name?"

He thought hard for a minute.

"The Legend League!" he said with enthusiasm. "No, wait. How about the Ghost Guard? Nah, that sounds like we patrol the coastline looking for spooks."

"Give it a rest," Billy advised. "We don't need a name."

"I've got it!" Chigger exclaimed. "Paranormal Patrol! That's it!"

"Hmm," Billy said thoughtfully. "That actually has a nice ring to it. What do you want to do, print up some business cards?"

"No, man, that'll be the name of our reality TV series," Chigger responded.

Soon they arrived back at Professor Buckhorn's office. He had two more topics for them to discuss.

"Chigger, Dr. Stevens insists on being called by his first name," Professor Buckhorn said. "That's unusual for him, but it makes it seem more like we're all equal partners in this."

"That's really great," Chigger said. "You guys are definitely smarter than me, but I have qualities of my own to contribute."

"I'm sure that's true," the professor admitted. "So I guess you can call me by my first name, too."

"That's what I'm talkin' about!" Chigger responded, jumping up. "Give me five."

He held his right hand up expecting James to slap it in the classic high-five move. When the man didn't respond, the boy dropped his arm.

"Too soon?" he asked. "Too forward?"

"It'll hurt your hand," James reminded the teen.

Chigger had forgotten all about his bandaged hands.

"And we're working together on a serious project, not hanging out," James replied. "No offense."

"None taken," Chigger said as he sat back down.

"So, team, when do we execute the plan?" James asked the group.

"As soon as possible," Wesley said. "Who knows who or what else might be attacked."

"It would help me a lot if we could hold off until my classes take their winter break," the professor said. "That way I can focus completely on this."

"When's that?" Wesley asked. "It's already mid-December."

"December eighteenth," James replied. "Not that long off really."

"That should work," Wesley said. "It'll take me that long to create eye-in-hand medallions for the five of us to wear. We've got to have those before we try to confront the serpent."

"Then it's settled," James said. "In the meantime, we'd better get mentally and physically prepared to meet the monster."

As they stood to leave, Chigger stepped into the midst of them.

"Paranormal Patrol dismissed!" he said in a military-style voice.

Everyone ignored him.

Billy drove Chigger home and headed back to his own place. He felt it was time to check in with his grandmother and maybe the Falcon Priest. Chigger had raised a good point earlier that day. Would Awinita and the priest be able to appear at exactly the right time? Would the guy who'd been dead for a thousand years really be able to speak the magic words using Billy's vocal chords? He wasn't sure.

That night he was restless. Sleep didn't come easily and he woke up several times after disturbing dreams. At around three a.m. he heard a familiar buzzing in his ears, a sign that Awinita might be nearby. Billy sat up. Soon his grandmother's glowing form came into view at the foot of his bed.

"Your worries have reached us," Awinita said. "The Falcon Priest has something to tell you."

The glowing form of the much taller Falcon Priest came into view. Billy had first seen this spirit at Spiral Mounds. At the time, he was so amazed by what was happening that he hadn't noticed what the spirit man looked like, but now he could really observe him.

His jet-black hair was framed by a multicolored headdress of feathers. The feathers fanned out on the back of his head looking like rays of sunshine. An animal skin was draped over his broad shoulders, and he wore a thick necklace made of square shell pieces. A leather belt covered with jewels was wrapped around his waist. The belt held up a deerskin robe that covered him down to his knees.

"Ancient peoples always paid attention to the stars and planets," the priest said. "The yearly timing of movements and alignments was of utmost importance. Everything we did was governed by the heavens. Our mounds and temples were built to line up with the sun, moon, and certain stars at important times of the year."

"So what about the timing for the ceremony to seal the serpent in the underground lake?" Billy asked. "Is there a best time for that?"

"Absolutely," the spirit priest replied. "The shortest day of sunlight is when it must be done. That day, which you call the winter solstice, approaches."

"December twenty-first," Billy said. "I only hope the beast doesn't hurt anyone before then. Can't we do it any sooner?"

"I wouldn't advise it," the glowing man said. "The risk of failure is too high any other time. On the winter solstice, late in the afternoon, the sun's rays shine directly into the mouth of the cave. The lower cavern will be well lit."

"All right, I'll tell the team," Billy said.

"And the diamond in the top of the staff you'll be holding will be at its most powerful," the Falcon Priest added. “We’ll need as much power as possible to hypnotize the serpent.”

“And there’s no doubt we can pull this off?” Billy asked, echoing Chigger’s question.

“There *is* one additional process you must learn to ensure our success,” the priest said. “It was necessary to wait until the proper time to bring it up.”

“Waiting for the stars to align are we?” Billy said jokingly.

“It’s good that you attempt humor,” the priest said. “You will probably need it to survive in the presence of the serpent.”

That statement drained all the humor right out of Billy.

“Survival is good,” he said nervously. “I like survival.”

At that moment, the spirit forms of four more men came into view. Each had a smaller version of the feathered headdress worn by the Falcon Priest. They all wore short robes made of animal skins.

“You must lie down so that my assistants can perform their duties,” the priest said to Billy.

Without knowing what was about to happen, Billy lay down in the middle of his bed.

"What are we doing?" Billy asked.

"Performing the spirit-travel ritual," the priest replied. "Your spirit must know how to leave its body for a short time so that I may live there in its place. Otherwise, I can't use your vocal chords to speak the sacred language. And the words must be said out loud."

"Wait a minute," Billy protested, sitting back up. "The last time I left my body, I was dying. Once was enough for me."

"Relax, Billy," Awinita said. "You'll be just fine. I won't let anything bad happen to you."

"Listen to your grandmother, young man," the priest said. "We are only here to help. You are about to learn the art of spirit travel. Soon you will take part in returning the beast to his underwater prison. Once these two rarest of tasks are achieved, you will be the only medicine man living to have done so."

Billy was now realizing the full meaning of the events he'd been part of. At the stomp grounds last September, he had a vision of climbing a ladder. Grandpa Wesley said that ladder represented the steps he would take to become a Cherokee medicine man. Billy could never in a million years have imagined where those steps would lead.

He lay down on his bed and waited for what was to come.

CHAPTER 7

Out of Body

Billy heard buzzing, which gradually grew louder and louder. As it did, it sounded more like humming. The four helpers moved to the four corners of Billy's bed. Billy realized the humming was coming from them.

The humming soon turned into a melody, a song that Billy recognized. It sounded a lot like the one sung by Cherokees every year at the Live Oak Stomp Grounds, where he and Wesley went on Labor Day. The old medicine man in charge of the stomp dance said it was one of the oldest songs the Cherokees knew. And here it was again being hummed by the spirits of thousand-year-old Mound Builder Indians. Wow!

The four helpers reached out toward Billy. One placed his hand under the boy's right foot. Another hand moved under his left foot. The two spirits near Billy's head reached under his shoulders.

At that point the humming moved into Billy's body. It became physical. It made him feel like his body was now humming the song. Strange. The vibration got faster and louder. Billy thought he might fall apart at any minute.

Then the Falcon Priest began speaking. No, it was more like chanting. The chanting was in a strange language Billy had never heard. It wasn't Cherokee, but it did contain a few words that seemed a little familiar.

At a signal from the Falcon Priest, the four helpers lifted Billy from the bed. The teen felt himself rise up supported by the hands of the helpers. He continued to rise and rise until he almost reached the ceiling. Just when Billy thought he was about to smash into the ceiling, he passed through it. That's when he realized that his physical body was still in bed.

Billy began to panic. He was just about to try to escape from the helpers when he saw his grandmother floating beside him. That calmed him down. She smiled.

Soon he and Awinita floated above his house. The helpers turned him over so he could look down at the ground below him. That's when he saw the Falcon Priest up ahead of him. Immediately Billy and the other six transparent spirit forms began racing away, heading south.

Soon they slowed down above a river. Billy looked closely and saw that they were about to reach the cave that once held the serpent captive. The flying group dropped down to the ledge at the mouth of the cave.

Continuing to move, they drifted into the cave. They quickly reached a fork in the path that divided it in two. The right path led down to the dark lake that once held the Horned Serpent. The left path led up through the white crystal room. The four helpers guided Billy along the upward path.

When they reached the white crystal room, the Falcon Priest and Awinita were already there waiting.

"We've brought you here, Billy, for a reason," the priest said. "Remember these images that you and your friend discovered?"

Billy looked again at the images scratched into the walls. It showed two groups of people separated by a central figure. The figure in the middle of the two groups was half man, half hawk. Billy now knew that was the Falcon Priest.

"Why do the people on the left side look sharp and clear?" Billy asked. "And why do the people on the right look all fuzzy? Chigger and I couldn't figure that out."

"The people on the left are alive and living on earth," Awinita answered. "And the people on the right are spirits. The Falcon Priest, in the middle, is communicating between the two."

Billy thought about that for a moment. Then he realized something.

"That's what you and I did when Luther brought a message for Uncle John," Billy said to his grandmother excitedly. "That's sort of what happens every time you visit me too."

"Now you've got the picture," Awinita said.

"That's part of the job of the Falcon Priest," the priest said. "I believe people in modern society call it being a medium."

"You're right," Billy said. "I remember seeing a woman on TV who does this all the time."

"So as you step into your role as Falcon Priest for modern times, this will become a regular part of your activities," the priest said.

"Wait. What?"

"That's right," the spirit priest confirmed. "You are to become the Falcon Priest for this age. You and your grandfather on earth will work with people in the physical world. Your grandmother will work with spirits in this world. Together, the three of you will help people connect with their loved ones and reconnect with their true selves. That is, if you want to."

Billy began feeling odd. In his mind he saw flashes of his body back home in bed. His physical body seemed to be calling to him. It needed something.

"You are getting a signal from your physical body," the spirit priest observed. "We must get you back. But before we go, there is one more thing for you to see."

Billy tried to focus on staying in the crystal cave.

"Your Dr. Stevens did indeed make an important discovery," the priest continued.

"The image of the Eye of God within the Hand of Man is one of the most powerful symbols there is."

"Good to know," Billy said. "But I'm fading fast. My body is calling to me."

"Look up quickly," the Falcon Priest instructed.

Billy looked up at the ceiling of the small space they were in. There, etched in the ceiling of the little room was that same symbol. The eye-in-hand picture he'd seen in Augustus's office.

"Make sure your grandfather finishes those medallions before you return here to face the serpent," the spirit priest said. "Their power will surely protect you."

With those words, Billy felt himself being pulled back to his physical body. Within seconds he felt himself merge back with the flesh. He lay still for a few seconds trying to feel what it was that was so important. He finally realized what it was. He had to pee.

"Really?" he said aloud, talking to his body as he got up to go to the bathroom. "You made me leave the most incredible experience of my life so I could drain my bladder? That's just pathetic."

The following morning in the family kitchen, Billy spoke to his father.

"I know when we're supposed to recapture the serpent in the cave," he said.

Professor Buckhorn, who was reading the morning paper, looked up when he realized what Billy was saying.

"Did you have a visitation last night?" he asked his son.

Billy nodded as he poured himself a cup of coffee.

"Don't keep me in suspense," his father said, dropping the paper. "When?"

"Winter solstice," Billy answered between sips of the hot liquid. "The afternoon of December twenty-first."

"That's perfect," the professor said after doing a few mental calculations. "We'll be on winter break at the college. That's good for Dr. Stevens too. Uh, I mean Augustus."

"What's good for Dr. Stevens?" Billy's mother said as she entered the kitchen and headed for the stove.

Billy repeated what he'd said to his father.

"Mom, I need you to sit down," Billy said in a calm voice. "There's something I have to tell you."

Puzzled, Mrs. Buckhorn sat down next to her husband at the breakfast table. Then Billy proceeded to tell his parents about his visit from the Falcon Priest and what the spirit had said about his own future.

Both parents were silent. Billy thought maybe they didn't believe him. Or maybe they weren't paying attention.

"I held my tongue when I first heard the wild tale about this big snake," his mother said. "And again when your father said he believed this story. I didn't express my opinion or my feelings."

Billy and his father just looked at her. Where was this going?

"But a woman who is a mother and wife has to speak when she hears that her husband and son are planning to confront this dangerous creature," she concluded. "Now I must ask if you two have gone absolutely mad."

"Rebecca, you don't seem to—" her husband began.

"Never in my life have I heard such crazy talk!" she said interrupting him. Standing up, she began to pace back and forth in the kitchen.

"I don't know if this creature is a figment of your imaginations," she continued, "or if you've been eating too many of Wesley's funny herbs from the garden. But this stuff has got to stop!"

She gave them both a harsh look and then stormed out of the room. Father and son were silent for a moment.

"She'll come around," Billy's dad finally said. "Look at me. I was once a die-hard materialist, only able to believe what the senses could perceive or what the instruments of science could measure."

"I'm not so sure she will," Billy said, pouring himself another cup of coffee.

"She'll eventually learn to accept it, just like Augustus has," the professor said. "Especially when she sees the video and pictures I'm going to shoot as the serpent comes back to the cave."

CHAPTER 8
Serpent Repellant

The day before the winter solstice, four of the five members of the Paranormal Patrol gathered at Dr. Stevens's house. The team had gear to pack and plans to make. Chigger, who was nervous and excited, chattered a mile a minute.

"I knew you guys would come around," he said. "Paranormal Patrol is the perfect name for this group."

"We're calling ourselves by that name as a joke," Billy said with a laugh. "It's too ridiculous to take seriously."

"Joke or not, it's what the professor and the scientist are calling us," Chigger said. "Isn't that right, Digger?"

"Please call me Augustus," the archaeologist said as he packed supplies in a box. "I don't like the name Digger."

"I like it, though," Chigger replied. "Augustus is too long and sounds like you're the king of Rome or something. Digger rhymes with Chigger, so it sounds like we could be pals."

Dr. Stevens thought about that for a moment and then reached a conclusion.

"All right then, young man," he said at last. "You may call me Digger. The rest of you," he said, speaking to the group, "shall continue calling me Augustus."

Chigger reached out his hand toward the man.

"I'm happy to make your acquaintance, Digger," the boy said. "I'm Chigger."

The two laughed as they shook hands.

"So to answer your question, I've labeled all the gear we're taking with the letters PP, for Paranormal Patrol," Augustus said. "It's easy to write and takes up less space on the labels."

"See?" Chigger said in a childish taunting voice. He was looking at Billy.

"But we would never use that name in public," Billy's dad, the professor, said as he finished packing a box. "It's a silly name."

He carried the box out to the van, which was parked in back of the house next to Dr. Stevens's boat.

Chigger looked absolutely deflated.

"Well, I still like it," he said as he finished stuffing freeze-dried food packets in a backpack. "Paranormal Patrol is just the greatest name in the history of names."

"Now we're ready to load the most important items of all," Augustus said. "The falcon cape and diamond staff."

He removed a large piece of the floor near the back of his office, revealing a hidden space underneath. A metal ladder led down to an underground vault. He climbed down the steps and turned on a light. The rest of the team watched from above.

"This is why the serpent couldn't find the diamond," Augustus said.

Turning around in the tight space, he reached out and spun the dial on a combination lock. Although this safe was built into the wall of the underground space, it reminded Billy of the safe in the shed behind Wesley's house.

"As soon as we're loaded up here, we'll head to Grandpa's house," Billy said. "He's expecting us in about an hour."

With one final spin of the lock, the safe was open. Augustus pulled out a long tube that held the cape and staff that he'd stored in the safe. He handed the tube up to Billy.

"Ever since I was attacked by the serpent, I've stored the cape and diamond staff in this new tube," Augustus said as he climbed back up the ladder. "It's lined with lead. I think that has made it hard for the beast to find the diamond."

"Good idea," Billy's dad said as he carried the tube to the van.

Within half an hour, the team had the van loaded and the boat trailer hooked up.

"Off to Grandpa's house we go," Chigger said excitedly as he jumped in the van.

When they arrived at Wesley's place, the elder was not waiting out front as expected. Billy tried the front door and found it open. He stepped inside while the rest of the team waited on the front porch.

"Grandpa," Billy called several times as he walked through the old house. As he passed through the kitchen, he heard the faint words "out here" coming from the backyard.

Stepping out the back door, Billy saw his grandfather in the field in the back of his house. The elderly medicine man was picking up broken pieces of wood that were scattered through the tall grass. Wesley was stacking the pieces in a pile.

Then Billy looked toward the woods farther away. There, where Wesley's shed once stood, was only the bank safe. It was lying on its side. Scratch marks scarred its surface.

"What happened?" Billy yelled as he ran toward his grandfather. "Are you all right?"

"Yeah, I'm fine," Wesley replied as Billy reached him. "What a mess. Good thing I finished making our eye-in-hand medallions."

He pointed toward the safe using his lips, as many older Natives did.

"Our serpent friend put in an appearance this morning," he said. "He was after the dark crystal."

"He didn't attack you, did he?" Billy asked as he helped Wesley pick up pieces of wood.

"No," his grandfather answered. "I was just finishing up the last medallion when I heard a loud crash from back here. Still holding the piece in my hand, I ran to see what had happened. That's when I saw him."

For the first time, Billy noticed the withered trail of grass heading off to the east.

"He had already destroyed the shed and was trying to break open the safe," Wesley continued. "He heard me coming and spun around to face me. Boy, is he big! And scary!"

"What did you do?" Billy asked.

"The same thing Dr. Stevens did," Wesley replied. "Without thinking, I held up my hands as if they could somehow protect me from the beast. I forgot I was holding the eye-in-hand medallion. The beast quickly pulled back. That's when I realized I was holding the medallion. The serpent tried to come at me from the side. When I turned the medallion toward him, he pulled back again."

"So that image really does repel the thing," Billy said.

"After that, he just gave up and slithered away," Wesley said, completing his story.

Just then, Billy's dad approached from the house.

"What's going on out here?" he asked. "We need to get going."

Billy gave his father a quick summary of what had taken place.

"I think we should load up and get out of here before it comes back," Professor Buckhorn said. "We'll come back later and help you clean up after the beast is no longer a threat."

Agreeing with his son's suggestion, Wesley opened the overturned safe and took out the pouch that held the dark crystal. Then the three Buckhorns went back in the house. Wesley grabbed his overnight bag and his medicine satchel. With a quick look around the house, he locked the front door. The team was now complete, and off they went in the van.

After hearing what had gone on behind Wesley's house, the group rode for a while in silence. Each member of the team was realizing the dangerous nature of their expedition. Was this going to be harder than they had imagined? What if the beast had other powers no one knew about?

Wesley began singing an old Cherokee warrior song. The words spoke of strength and victory. In the old days, the men in a war party would sing this before facing an enemy. Billy recognized the song. It was one he'd heard his grandfather sing before. He joined in. Billy's dad also remembered hearing Wesley sing it long ago and followed along as best he could.

Wesley kept singing the song over and over. So Chigger and Augustus picked up on the tune and began singing along as well. Wesley was the only one who knew exactly what the words meant. But all of them felt the strength of that song. And each one of them became more certain of his mission with every passing mile.

Arriving at the boat landing on the river, the team transferred their gear to the boat. Quickly they shoved off, heading south down the river. They reached the campsite near the cave in the middle of the afternoon.

Everyone on the team was eager to get started setting up.

"Hold on, everybody," Wesley said as he took his medicine satchel out of the boat. "First things first. Let's form a small circle."

He set his bag down on the ground and opened it. The other team members gathered around him.

"All great endeavors should begin with prayer," Wesley said as he removed his pipe and tobacco from the satchel. "We are here by the river, so when we've finished, we'll purify ourselves in the water."

Augustus, the scientist, was not sure what to expect. He didn't begin most of his projects with a prayer. But, as a loyal member of the Paranormal Patrol, he followed along.

Wesley placed a small amount of natural tobacco in the pipe and lit it. Then, in the Cherokee language, he prayed on their behalf asking Creator to bless their task and protect them from harm. After taking four puffs of the pipe, he passed it on. And so it went around the circle.

When all the tobacco had been smoked, Wesley and Billy sat down and removed their shoes. The others did the same. Wesley and his grandson waded into the shallow part of the river. The others watched.

"Cherokees call this 'going to the water,'" Wesley said. "It purifies us inside and out."

He and Billy demonstrated the process. Each of them cupped their hands together and scooped up a handful of water. Then, as Wesley recited another Cherokee prayer, they threw the handfuls of water over their shoulders. This was done four times. The rest of the team did the same thing.

"Now we're ready to do this thing," Wesley said, and led them back to the riverbank.

The first task was to have Chigger remove the dark crystal from its case. He would carry it around for a while. The team hoped this would reopen the beast's connection to the boy. While everyone else unloaded equipment and set up camp, Chigger walked around with the crystal. It wasn't long before he started feeling weird.

"I think something's happening," he said in a loud voice. "The stone is getting warm and beginning to glow. And I'm beginning to feel light-headed."

"Good," Wesley said. "Hopefully the serpent has learned of the gem's new location.

It's time for the next step. It's time to put the dark crystal back in its original place."

With Chigger and the crystal in front, the team climbed up the steps that led to the cave. They stood on the ledge at the cave's mouth and turned on their flashlights. Gathering all the courage he could, Chigger headed into the darkness.

All five team members walked down the lower path and headed for the stone door. Once they arrived, they watched Chigger place the crystal back on the pedestal. They waited to see if anything would happen. Would the gem begin to glow brighter? Or would a strange wind come blowing into the cavern?

Nothing changed. So the team headed back to their camp.

Little did they know that something *had* actually happened. An unseen signal went out from that dark stone. The bats that had lived in that cave felt it. So did the serpent. And so did the ghost of the Dark Priest.

For the bats, it was like a homing beacon. They somehow knew it was time to return to the cave. For the Dark Priest, it was his signal to guide the serpent back to gather up the stone. After all, it did belong to the serpent. And soon the serpent would once again do the Dark Priest's bidding.

As for Billy and the team, they could only hope that the beast would show up at the right time. But they had to be ready in case it came earlier or later than planned. So there was a twenty-four hour watch schedule set up. Each member of the team would take a four-hour shift. Around the clock someone would be on the lookout for the beast.

Before the first shift began, Wesley passed out the eye-in-hand medallions.

"Wear this at all times until we've completed our mission," he instructed. "Don't take it off to sleep, eat, or go to the bathroom."

Billy volunteered for the first watch. That way he'd be able to sleep most of the night and get plenty of rest. He had to be ready. Who knew when the serpent would actually show up? Who knew how soon he'd have to allow the spirit of the ancient Falcon Priest to possess him?

CHAPTER 9
Practice Makes Perfect

Billy's watch shift was uneventful. The rising moon shone brightly over the darkened landscape. The lookout position they used was the ledge above the campsite. From that spot, they could see both upriver and downriver for several miles. Chigger took the next watch.

He came to the ledge carrying an armload of snacks and his flashlight.

"All's quiet," Billy said as he let Chigger take his seat in the dirt.

Back at the camp, Billy took a few bites of an energy bar before curling up in his sleeping bag for the night. He hadn't realized just how tired he was until his head hit the pillow. He went out like a light.

Around midnight Billy started dreaming. He was back on top of the ancient mound. This was the same mound he'd dreamed of before. This time the Falcon Priest was with him. And two of the helpers who had lifted Billy out of his body were nearby.

"Am I dreaming?" Billy asked.

"Yes and no," the priest answered. "Your brain is asleep and dreaming, but your mind is awake. This is so you can practice leaving your body one more time."

The priest began humming. It was the same song Billy heard the first time he left his body. The teen hummed along this time as the helpers moved in closer. Everyone was humming. They lifted the boy off the ground and held him above their heads.

Then all four of them floated upward. They drifted away from the mound and out over the land below. Billy looked down. Suddenly he was no longer above the mound. He was now hovering over his own physical body. He was beginning to get used to this experience.

"That's the idea," the priest said. "The more you practice, the better you will become."

The priest nodded to the helpers. The two slowly removed their hands from under Billy's arms. He continued to float. The helpers moved a little farther away. Billy continued to float.

"Now what?" he asked.

"Now you begin to learn the skills of spirit travel," the priest said. "You practice the art of leaving and returning to your body. You practice the art of moving from place to place. It all takes practice."

Billy tried flapping his arms like a bird. He felt silly and he didn't move an inch. Then he tried to swim through the air like a swimmer would move through water. After a few useless strokes, he still hadn't moved an inch. He looked to the priest for help. The man was grinning from ear to ear. He enjoyed watching Billy flailing around.

"It won't be like physically moving," he said. "It is all about focusing your attention."

Billy didn't get it.

"Think hard about a place you want to go or someone you want to see," the priest advised. "Picture that in your mind."

Billy shut everything out. Then he thought of Chigger up at the lookout point. Immediately he felt a blur of movement. It wasn't like flying. It was more like stretching. One part of him instantly floated near Chigger. The rest of Billy caught up a split second later.

Billy looked around and found that he was floating out in front of the ledge. Chigger sat in front of him at the mouth of the cave—fast asleep. Billy tried to wake him up.

"Wake up, sleepyhead," Billy said, but got no response. "I said wake up!" he shouted. Still no response.

"You're supposed to be watching out for the beast!" he yelled as loud as he could. Still nothing.

"He can't hear you," the priest said. He was watching the whole thing from a few feet away. "You are invisible to him. You are yelling with your thoughts, not your voice."

"Oh yeah," Billy said. "I forgot."

"Now you know why I must take over your body and your vocal chords to speak the sacred words," the spirit man said. "The words must be spoken aloud in the physical realm."

"Got it," Billy replied.

Then the Falcon Priest and his helpers moved Billy's spirit body away. In two quick blinks they were back at the ancient mound site. That's where Billy's dream began.

"Where is this place?" Billy asked as they settled down on top of the mound.

"The better question is not only where but also when," the priest answered. "Time and place have different meanings in the spirit world. This place is the Temple Mound, and the time is about one thousand years in your past."

Once again Billy did not understand what he was being told.

"Huh?" he thought.

"There will be plenty of time to grasp these ideas later," the priest said. "You will learn all there is to know about spirit travel and the other worlds. For now we must focus on the job at hand."

"Of course," Billy said.

"You may return to your body," the priest said. "I think you are ready for the ceremony to recapture the serpent."

With that, Billy zoomed back to the campsite. He jolted awake, back in his physical body. Feeling a little dazed, he sat up in his sleeping bag. Everyone else was asleep. He thought of Chigger, who was also asleep at his post.

Billy climbed up the steps in the face of the cliff. He stepped onto the ledge in front of the cave. There was Chigger, fast asleep, just as he'd seen him earlier.

"Wake up, sleepyhead," he said to his friend. No response.

"I said wake up!" he shouted as he'd done before. This time there was an immediate response.

"What? Where?" Chigger said as he jumped up off the ground. "Who's there?"

Billy broke out a big belly laugh that went on and on.

Then he said, "You've been sleeping on the job."

Chigger finally woke up enough to realize what was happening.

"So I fell asleep," Chigger admitted. "It's not that funny."

Then a thought struck him.

"How did you know I was asleep?" Chigger asked.

"I was up here earlier and I saw you sleeping," Billy said, still chuckling. "I even tried to wake you up, but you couldn't hear me."

"Why didn't I hear you?" Chigger said. "I heard you just now. Why wouldn't I have heard you before?"

"Because I wasn't in my body," Billy said. "I was practicing spirit travel."

Chigger blinked. He was trying hard to get what Billy was saying. Then his eyes lit up.

"You were spying on me?" he said as he realized what Billy could do. "You can spy on people without them knowing it?"

"I hadn't thought of it like that," Billy answered. "I guess I can."

"Do you know what the government would do if they knew about this?" Chigger said.

"Down, boy," Billy said. "You're having another fantasy attack."

"No, I'm serious," Chigger protested. "This could—"

"Enough, already," Billy interrupted. "I'm going back to bed."

He reached into his back pocket and pulled out a small can of energy drink he'd brought with him. He handed the can to Chigger.

"Maybe this will help you stay awake," he said and climbed back down the stone stairs.

CHAPTER 10
Winter Solstice

The Paranormal Patrol team members took turns keeping watch the rest of the night. Nothing much happened except that clouds rolled in. Billy awoke to gray skies. No sun. And it was the big day: winter solstice.

Billy's father had explained that the summer and winter solstices were often tied together in tribal cultures. During a ceremony on the summer solstice, some tribes used a clear crystal to capture the sun's rays. That was on June twenty-first, the longest day of sunlight. People believed the sun to be most powerful then.

That crystal would be stored away until the winter solstice. During a ceremony on or near December twenty-first, those rays would be released from the crystal on the shortest day. This would ensure that the sun would begin its new cycle. Its power would increase as the days got longer.

"The weather forecast didn't say anything about clouds for today," James said. "I hope it doesn't hamper our plans."

"The Falcon Priest said the diamond was most powerful on this day," Billy said. "So I think the ceremony will still work."

Augustus finished his turn on the watch. He came down to the camp to have breakfast.

"Nothing much to report," he said as he was eating his freeze-dried eggs. "Just that I started seeing bats before sunrise this morning."

"What?" Billy sat up straight, alarmed by this news.

"They came from all directions," Augustus continued. "In little groups. I had to stay low to keep from getting hit as they flew into the cave."

"Why didn't you call us?" Wesley asked. He was also alarmed.

"I figured it was normal for bats to enter the cave at sunrise," Augustus replied. "Nobody ever said anything about bats. I was just watching for the serpent."

"Oh my gosh," Billy said as he stood up. "We'd better get ready."

Everyone but the scientist stood up.

"What's going on?" he asked with a puzzled face. "What did I miss?"

"The return of the bats means the beast is on its way," Chigger said. "They haven't been back to this cave since the day the serpent left. Everyone knows that." He shook his head as if this was the most obvious thing in the world.

Chigger grabbed the binoculars from near the campfire. Then he scrambled up the stone stairs as fast as he could. He stood on the ledge and looked upstream. He could see no signs of the serpent. What the team hoped to see was irregular movement in the middle of the river, a water trail that showed where the snake was swimming.

"No sign of it yet," Chigger yelled to the camp below.

"Keep watching," Wesley called up to him.

"Get behind that rock so he can't see you," Billy's father said. Then he began preparing his cameras in hopes of recording the event. Chigger hid behind a large rock on the ledge. He peered through the binoculars.

The professor brought two video cameras and one still camera. Everything was digital. He had already set up one video camera on a tripod. It had a wide-angle lens. It would capture everything from the river's edge to the mouth of the cave. He could start recording using a little remote control he kept in his pocket.

Wesley and Billy made their way to the upper crystal room inside the cave. Augustus had hidden the tube there so the cape and staff would be handy when needed. The team had also placed a cot in that room as part of their plan. Wesley helped Billy put on the cape. Then the teen lay down on the cot. When the final signal came, he would begin the process of leaving his body.

Wesley left the diamond staff inside the tube. The diamond was to remain hidden until the serpent had reached the bottom of the lower path.

Wesley made his way back down the upper path. He stood just inside the mouth of the cave so he'd hear Chigger's signal. He made sure he was out of sight.

Augustus took up his position as well. Even though he'd been told that bullets couldn't pierce the serpent's scales, he wanted to try. He had created a camouflaged hunting bunker at the edge of the river. This was located out of the way but near where the serpent would slither to reach the cave. The archaeologist did a final check of the ammo for the handgun and the rifle he'd brought. They were locked and loaded. He planned to shoot the beast if it escaped from the cave. That would only happen if the Falcon Priest's ceremony failed.

All was ready for the Uktena to arrive. The only thing the team needed now was some sunshine. That would guarantee their success.

Time passed. Everyone waited and watched. Chigger peered through the binoculars. The clouds continued to cover the sun. Wesley waited just inside the cave for the final signal.

At around two o'clock, Chigger checked the binoculars one more time. Starting in the water near their camp, he moved his view slowly upriver. He caught sight of a swirl of water. He paused to take a closer look. A turtle popped his head up. Chigger moved on.

About a hundred yards farther upstream, he saw another swirl. Probably another turtle, Chigger thought. He focused the lenses. The swirl continued to move downstream. Then Chigger saw a few shiny scales just under the water's surface. Then there was a long line of scales.

Suddenly the serpent's head rose out of the water. A few sprigs of underwater plants hung from his antlers. He licked the air with his very long tongue. Chigger jumped and nearly dropped the binoculars.

He put his fingers to the corners of his mouth and tried to whistle. That was supposed to be the signal to let the team know the beast had been spotted. But he couldn't make his mouth whistle. All that came out was a spitting noise. He tried again, but this time it only sounded like he was passing gas.

He turned toward the cave.

"It's coming!" he said in a loud whisper. "I saw it. It's coming."

Wesley nodded that he'd heard Chigger's warning. The elder headed immediately to the upper path to warn Billy.

Meanwhile, Chigger looked down toward the camp and repeated his warning. Billy's dad stood up from his hiding place and gave Chigger a thumbs-up. So did Augustus.

Chigger immediately headed for his designated hiding place. The plan called for him to help Billy's dad with the cameras. James turned on the first video camera, the one on the tripod. He held on to the other one so he could follow the beast into the cave. He gave Chigger the still camera.

In the upper room, Billy lay down on the cot and began humming the song the Falcon Priest taught him. In order for him to escape his body, he had to completely relax and wait for the vibrations to begin.

Soon the familiar humming sound came to his ear. This told him Awinita was standing by. Soon she and the Falcon Priest began to appear. Beside the priest were two spirit assistants. Again the assistants hummed their song. That started the vibrations that allowed Billy to leave his body.

The priest chanted and the assistants moved in to lift Billy's spirit body up. Once

Billy was out, he waited with Awinita. What they witnessed next seemed very strange. Stranger than anything else either one had experienced.

From out of nowhere, a ghostly being appeared in the upper room. He looked like the Falcon Priest. His spirit clothing was similar. His face was similar but distorted. But his spirit body was deformed. He seemed to be a poor imitation of the Falcon Priest.

This figure's appearance took the Falcon Priest by surprise. Billy watched as the two spirit beings confronted each other. Then Billy saw a flicker of recognition pulse through the Falcon Priest. He knew who the intruder was!

"The Dark Priest," Billy heard. The thoughts came from his teacher, the Falcon Priest.

But before the Falcon Priest could move or do anything else, the intruder thrust himself into Billy's physical body. Billy understood that the Dark Priest intended to possess him. Billy's spirit body began to feel heavy. His energy was draining. Awinita saw and felt what was happening to him.

Quickly, acting in unison, the Falcon Priest, his helpers, and Awinita surrounded Billy's body and moved in on the intruder. Humming a higher-pitched version of the Cherokee song Billy knew, they wrestled with the Dark Priest's ghost.

With so much energy swirling around him, Billy felt quite ill. Was it his spirit body or his physical body that felt that way? He couldn't tell. The two were mingled together. As the struggle continued, he remembered the warrior song his grandfather had sung in the van. With all the energy he could muster, he began humming that melody. Awinita felt it and joined in. She glowed more brightly, sending strong energy to Billy.

With this extra spiritual strength, Billy also began pushing against the Dark Priest. That extra push was what was needed. The intruder was thrust from Billy's physical body. Quickly the Falcon Priest blocked the uninvited guest from re-entering the body.

And then suddenly a bright ball of fiery energy shot out from the Falcon Priest's chest. It hit the Dark Priest like a cannonball.

The deformed entity flew backward, crashing against the cave's crystal wall. Without hesitating, the Falcon Priest threw an energy rope toward the intruder. The bright rope wrapped around the Dark Priest. To Billy it was almost like a cowboy roping a calf.

The Falcon Priest streaked up and away, with the Dark Priest tied in the rope dragging behind him. The two disappeared momentarily. Within a matter of seconds, the Falcon Priest reappeared.

"Who was that?" Billy asked. "What just happened?"

"No time for explanations," The Falcon Priest replied. "We have to begin the ceremony now."

Without further delay, the Falcon Priest's spirit body began getting smaller. He shrank to the size of Billy's body. Then he lay down on the cot, merging himself with Billy's body. Billy's spirit body somehow felt what the physical body was feeling. It looked and felt as though the priest had put on Billy's body like a suit—a Billy suit.

Then Billy's physical body stood up from the cot. But now that body seemed bigger, stronger. The priest's powerful presence was actually affecting the molecules in Billy's physical body.

The physical Billy began chanting the same chant the Falcon Priest had chanted before. At first, the words weren't clear. The priest's spirit was adapting to being inside a physical body for the first time in a thousand years. It took a little getting used to. Billy and Awinita were both amazed that this actually worked.

Wesley handed the tube that held the diamond staff to the priest in the Billy suit. Moving stiffly at first, the boy took the tube. He slung the strap over his shoulder.

And they waited.

CHAPTER 11
Casting the Spell

Down at the river, Augustus, Chigger, and James began to smell a foul odor. At about the same time, they heard splashes in the water. The Horned Serpent had arrived. The three humans froze in place and held their breath. They dared not move.

Soon the beast's head came up out of the water. He hissed as he studied his surroundings. He saw nothing that made him suspicious. The video camera sitting on its tripod was odd to the beast but not threatening, so he ignored it. He looked up toward the cave. That's where the unseen signal came from. The dark crystal called to him from there. Finally, the gem would be returned to its rightful place.

This was the first time either Chigger or Billy's dad had seen the creature. Its scales seemed to constantly change colors. Sometimes they were white; other times they seemed blue or green. And the antlers on top of his head almost looked like those of a deer. In the middle of the beast's forehead was an indention where the diamond used to sit. On either side of the indention glowed a red eye. The eyes were burning, filled with death.

Before exiting the water, the serpent extended his tongue and licked the air. As with all reptiles, this is where he had his sense of smell. That's when Chigger saw the beast's fangs and teeth, sharp and yellowed and dripping with saliva. Chigger shuddered at the sight.

Luckily, everyone in the Paranormal Patrol had rubbed themselves with dirt and green leaves. That prevented the serpent from detecting their human scents.

Satisfied that the coast was clear, the beast slithered out of the water and up the craggy cliff.

That's when Chigger finally remembered to send the second signal up to the crystal room. Dr. Stevens had run a small black wire from the campsite up the cliff. It continued into the upper room. To one end of the wire was attached a small trigger. On the other end of the wire was a red light. Chigger pushed the trigger, which turned on the light.

The Falcon Priest, wearing Billy's body, saw the signal. He knew the serpent was entering the cave. Time to take action. He quietly moved down the path toward the lower cavern.

Once the serpent had entered the cave, James and Chigger quietly climbed the stone stairs. They followed the beast into the darkness. But they had no trouble knowing where the beast was. Its fiery eyes glowed red. And as it slithered along, its scales crunched against the loose dirt on the cave floor. James began videotaping in the cave, using the camera's night vision.

Downward the beast moved toward its precious dark crystal. At last the stone was in his sight. Soon it would be rejoined to his tail.

At the same time, the Falcon Priest in Billy's body stepped out on the ledge. He removed the diamond staff from the tube. Holding the staff up over his head, he turned toward the west. He silently called to Grandfather Sun, asking the Old Man to appear. Then, loudly, he began to speak his ancient language. Again, he asked the Grandfather to shine forth.

Suddenly a wind arose from the west. The clouds above began churning and swirling. To the amazement of James and Chigger, layers of clouds began to part. Dark ones moved away, replaced by white fluffy ones. But they didn't fully part. They still blocked the sun.

Thankfully, enough light reached the diamond to activate it. It began to glow dimly.

At the same moment, down at the bottom of the path, the beast suddenly turned. He, too, felt the power of that gem as its brightness grew.

Quickly the Falcon Priest carried the staff down the lower path. As he did, he loudly proclaimed the sacred words. Upon seeing the brightly shining diamond and hearing the ancient words, the serpent fell under a spell. It was the same spell that had captured him so long ago. He stopped moving.

The spirit version of Billy hovered nearby, watching the action. It was very odd to see himself, his body, doing things without him. He was in two places at the same time! Until now, he believed that was impossible.

Chigger thought this would be a perfect time to take a picture. He pressed the camera's button. It was an automatic camera, so the flash unit popped up. A second later, its bright light flashed in the darkness. This startled everyone—even the serpent.

It awoke from the spell and looked around. Quickly the creature saw the diamond in the staff and headed toward it. The priest in the Billy suit started chanting the spell faster and louder.

Suddenly, the clouds in the sky finally parted. Rays of bright sunlight streamed into the lower area of the cave. A few of those rays struck the diamond. The gem ignited as if it had been set on fire. A heavenly brilliance filled the cavern.

The light reached the Horned Serpent and filled his eyes. He grew still as the chanting and the unearthly radiance filled his mind. The priest drew closer to the beast, chanting more powerfully with each step. Soon he was dangerously close to the monster. But by that time it was back under the priest's spell. The serpent stared blankly at the diamond.

The priest continued his chant and headed down the path. The beast remained fixated on the stone and followed the priest each step of the way. The priest led the beast through the open stone door. Turning to the right, the priest walked along a raised platform next to the lower lake. The beast slithered into the dark liquid with ease. Chigger remembered that the fluid was like a thick tea filled with herbs that made the serpent fall into a deep sleep. There, in that ancient sleepy-time tea, the Uktena floated in a daze.

The priest made his way back to the stone door in the cave and stood in front of it. Reading from the symbols carved into the stone, he began the sealing ceremony. His commanding voice echoed throughout the cavern.

Chigger looked up at the ceiling. The bat colony had settled back in its place. The bats, too, grew still and quiet as the chanting came to an end.

Just before voicing the final words of the spell, the priest stepped back from the door. He completed the ceremony with a closing word.

"*Aho*," he said, the way countless generations of Native people had ended prayers down through the centuries.

With that, the stone door swung shut all by itself. A sucking noise flowed from around the edges of the door. It sealed itself closed once again.

"It is finished," Billy the priest said, uttering words in English for the first and only time.

The diamond on the staff stopped glowing as the ancient stick fell to the cave floor. Billy's body collapsed on the floor beside it. James and Chigger were enveloped in darkness and engulfed in utter silence.

Neither one moved for a long moment. Finally, Chigger pulled a flashlight out of his pocket and turned it on. His first concern was the condition of his friend.

"Billy, are you all right?" he called as the beam of his light searched the floor.

In a few moments the light fell on Billy's unmoving body. Both James and Chigger rushed to him. James felt for a pulse on his son's neck. He touched the scar left on his son by the lightning strike four months earlier. The weblike scar pattern was hot to the touch. Upon a closer look, James saw that it was glowing. It looked like a hot net of lava had splattered on Billy's neck.

"Help me get him out of here," James told Chigger. "We've got to see what's wrong with his neck."

Together, the two Paranormal Patrol team members struggled to carry Billy out of the cave. They set him down on the ledge. Wesley and Augustus joined them as James felt for a pulse on the boy's wrist. Finally the man relaxed.

"I found a pulse," he reported. "It sounds strong and regular."

He looked more closely at the weblike pattern on his son's neck. It had stopped glowing, but it was still red. It looked like it had looked right after the lightning strike.

A few moments later, Billy stirred. He opened his eyes and found himself surrounded by the members of his team. He sat up and looked around.

"I'm back," he said with a smile. "Now that was some strange stuff."

"Are you all right?" James asked. "The scar on your neck is glowing."

Billy reached up to feel the scar.

"Ow!" he yelped. "It's sore. It feels like it did when I was recovering in the hospital. Energy from the Falcon Priest must've caused that."

He stood up under his own power and everyone breathed a sigh of relief. Then a realization began to settle in. Their mission was complete. The plan had actually worked!

"I've had enough of this place for a while," Billy said. "I think it's time we get out of here."

"First we have to decide what we're going to do about this place," Augustus said. "We can't just leave it for someone else to accidentally discover."

They all knew he was right. The serpent must never be released again.

"Can't we dynamite the cave entrance?" Chigger suggested. "That should do it."

"We can't," Billy said. "We need to have access to a part of the cave."

"What for?" Chigger asked.

"I learned something while I was in the upper room with the Falcon Priest," Billy said. "I think I'm supposed to put that space to use."

"How are you supposed to put it to use?" Billy's dad asked.

"Billy's going to reconnect people to their loved ones who've died," Wesley answered. "Just like the original Falcon Priest did. Billy is now his apprentice."

They all looked at Wesley.

"And you know this how?" James asked his father.

"You forget that I've been connecting with the spirit world for a long time," Wesley reminded him. "Not like Billy can, but in my own way. So I pick up on things."

"Grandpa's right," Billy confirmed. "They're expecting me to carry on that work. It's a little like what they've been doing at the Live Oak Stomp Grounds."

"But this is more powerful," Wesley continued. "It's from the original source."

The Paranormal Patrol was silent. They needed time to absorb these new ideas. Quietly they set about the task of packing up to head back home. The decision about sealing the lower cavern would have to wait.

CHAPTER 12
Nothing to Show

When the team got back to Dr. Stevens's house, they took time to review the photos and video that had been shot. James played back the tape from the tripod-mounted video camera. Oddly, there was nothing on the tape but washed out, distorted images. It looked like the tape had been placed near a magnet.

On the other video camera there were only snowy, grainy shadows. James and Augustus were heartbroken. They'd expected to have visual proof of the creature to show the academic world. Now there was nothing.

"Let's check the still camera," James said with a hint of hope.

A quick check of that camera revealed only a single image. It was the one Chigger took inside the lower cavern when the camera flashed. What it showed was Billy wearing the falcon cape and holding the diamond staff. No Horned Serpent.

But as they looked more closely at the image, they did realize one thing. Billy looked a lot like the half-man, half-bird image that had been etched into the wall of the upper crystal room. Billy seemed somehow larger and more majestic than usual. And his eyes were on fire! It wasn't the usual camera red-eye caused by the flash. His eyes glowed with golden energy.

"The Falcon Priest's energy was radiating from Billy's body," Wesley said. "His power is a supernatural force that changed Billy's physical appearance for a while."

"With no photo and no video, we have no proof," Augustus said. "I think it's a sign."

"A sign of what?" Billy asked.

"That some things in this world are best kept secret," Billy's dad said, realizing what the scientist was getting at. "There'll be no press conference to announce the greatest archeology find in modern times. We won't be writing any reports to publish in academic journals."

"Your father and I have come to respect what you and Wesley are doing," Augustus said, continuing with the idea started by James.

"And you need to operate without a lot of media attention. It works best that way."

Another moment of silence settled over the group. Each person was lost in his own thoughts.

"Okay, there's one thing that's been bugging me ever since we found out the Horned Serpent was more than a legend," Chigger said. "Who created it? Where did it come from?"

"Every culture has its stories of monsters that lived long ago," James said, sounding every bit like the college professor he was. "Maybe humans have believed these things for so long that they came into being."

"According to the Old Testament of the Bible, God created a great and terrible sea monster called the leviathan," Wesley said unexpectedly.

"When did you start reading the Bible?" Billy asked.

"When your grandma Awinita died," Grandpa answered. "It's hers. I keep it on the nightstand next to my bed. I read it every night. You'd be surprised by what can be found in there."

"I thought you only believed in Cherokee culture," Chigger observed.

"Spiritual teachings come from many places," Wesley replied. "But Cherokee ways are still closest to my heart."

"I learn something new about you every day, old man," James said with admiration. "What does the Old Testament say about this leviathan?"

"'In that day, the Lord with his great and powerful sword shall punish leviathan, the piercing serpent,'" Wesley quoted. "'Even leviathan that crooked serpent; and he shall slay the dragon that is in the sea. Isaiah 27.' There's another one from the Book of Job I could give you."

"No, no," James protested. "That one is plenty."

"Then there's a Cherokee legend that says the Horned Serpent was created by an angry medicine man who turned a human being into the Uktena and banished him to the Underworld."

"Stop, you're hurting my brain," James pleaded. "I've seen and heard more than enough the last few days to completely rearrange my view of the world. I need a break."

Yet another moment of silence came upon the team. In their minds, they were all updating their views of the physical world as well as the spirit world.

After they unloaded all the gear from the van and the boat, the team broke up. Each one headed back to his normal life. But none of them would be the same.

At home, James and Billy gave Mrs. Buckhorn a full report. With each new turn of the story, she gasped in amazement. At the end, she was sworn to secrecy. No one was to ever know about the very real appearance of the legendary beast.

"No one would believe any of it anyway," she admitted.

Before drifting off to sleep, Billy heard the familiar humming in his ears. Soon his grandmother's transparent form came into view at the foot of his bed. And his great-grandfather Bullseye showed up, too.

"I'm very proud of you," Awinita said. "Your victory has created a positive ripple effect throughout our worlds."

"So who was that intruder who tried to take over my body and what was he doing?" Billy asked. "I can't take the suspense."

"The Falcon Priest explained that to us," Bullseye answered. "That was the Dark Priest trying to get into your body before the Falcon Priest could."

"Why would he want to do that?" Billy said.

"Because a thousand years ago, he was the Serpent King, the leader of a cult that worshipped the beast," Awinita responded. "It's a long story, but the short version is that he was the Falcon Priest's own twin brother. He was exiled from the Mound Builder society. The two brothers became mortal enemies."

"So he wanted to be the one to control the serpent," Billy said, putting some of the details together in his mind. "Maybe he thought he could beat his brother this time."

"Very good," Bullseye said. "But the Dark Priest has been cast even more deeply into the lower regions. Hopefully you won't be hearing anything from him for quite a while."

Billy thought hard for a long moment. He was trying to absorb all that had occurred.

"Who would have ever thought a sixteen-year-old Cherokee would be involved in such things?" Billy said. "I'm still trying to get used to all of this."

"In time you'll get used to it," Awinita said. "This *is* just the beginning."

"What happened to the Falcon Priest?" Billy asked. "He just sort of disappeared after the door was resealed."

"He had places to go, things to do," Grandma said. "He said he'll meet you at the top of the Temple Mound on the summer solstice."

"The mound I saw in my dream?"

"That's the one," Awinita answered. "Do you know where it is?"

"No, I don't," Billy admitted. "When I asked him where it was, he said I should ask when it was."

"Because that mound was the center of his civilization a thousand years ago," Grandma said. "Now it's a national park in Illinois. In his time, the priest said it was called Solstice City. The winter and summer solstice ceremonies were held there."

"So I'm supposed to meet him there on June twenty-first?" Billy asked.

"Yes," his grandmother said. "And that's all I know about it. You'll have to go there yourself to find out the rest."

"Okay," Billy replied with a big yawn. He was feeling tired all the way down to his bones. His ability to maintain contact with his grandmother was fading.

"Sleep well, young man," she said.

"See you again soon," Bullseye added.

And they both dissolved into nothingness.

Soon Billy fell into a deep, restful sleep. Much had happened in his life during the past few months, many nearly unbelievable things.

He had a feeling much more was to come.

ABOUT THE AUTHOR

Gary Robinson, a writer and filmmaker of Cherokee and Choctaw Indian descent, has spent more than twenty-five years working with American Indian communities to tell the historical and contemporary stories of Native people in all forms of media. His television work has aired on PBS, Turner Broadcasting, Ovation Network, and others. His nonfiction books, *From Warriors to Soldiers* and *The Language of Victory*, reveal little-known aspects of American Indian service in the US military from the Revolutionary War to modern times. He has also written three other teen novels, *Thunder on the Plains*, *Tribal Journey*, and *Little Brother of War*, and two children's books that share aspects of Native American culture through popular holiday themes: *Native American Night Before Christmas* and *Native American Twelve Days of Christmas*. He lives in rural central California.